The Lambton Curse

by

Malachy Doyle

Illustrated by Dylan Gibson

To find out more about Malachy and his books, please visit:
www.malachydoyle.com

LONDON BOROUGH OF WANDSWORTH	
9030 00000 8434 0	
Askews	25-Feb-2010
JF C DOYL	£5.99
	WWX0005915/0076

First published in 2010 in Great Britain by
Barrington Stoke Ltd
18 Walker St, Edinburgh, EH3 7LP

www.barringtonstoke.co.uk

ISBN: 978-1-84299-757-4

Printed in Great Britain by Bell & Bain Ltd

Contents

Chapter 1
Young Lambton

It was early morning in the kitchen of Lambton Hall, but the cook was already hard at work.

"Are you on your way to church, Young Lambton?" she asked, as a boy came into the room.

"No chance, you old bag – I'm off fishing!" said he, grabbing a chunk of the pie that the woman had just taken from the oven.

"Crikey, that's hot!" he cried, tossing it from hand to hand and trying to get out of the kitchen before she caught hold of him.

He wiggled this way and that and he'd nearly escaped, but there was Lord Lambton, his father, standing in the doorway. "Give that back, boy! Go and put on your Sunday clothes and come with me to church."

"Not likely!" He stuffed the red-hot pie in his mouth and ducked between his father's legs. "I'll see you later, old man!"

****

"Damn and blast!" muttered Young Lambton. He was down by the river, well away from all the spoil-sports. He'd been there at least an hour, the fish weren't biting, and his hook had just caught on a lump of weed.

"Damn and double blast!" he yelled ten minutes later, flinging his rod down on the grassy bank. "Those stupid fish must still be asleep." But then he saw a ripple on the water. Was it a fish? Could it really be a fish?

"I'll give it one more go, and that's it," he said to himself, putting a little white grub on his hook and casting in. Straight away, there was a mighty tug on the end of the line.

"Got you, you beggar!" His rod bent like a bow. "One hell of a fine salmon, by the feel of you."

Whatever he'd caught didn't want to come out, but Young Lambton wasn't one to give up without a fight. He pulled and he tugged, he tugged and he pulled and at last, with a mighty splash, he dragged it from the water.

"Hell fire!" he shouted. "What on earth are you?"

For there, wiggling and jiggling on the end of the line, was the ugliest, most evil-looking monster the boy had ever seen. It was as long as his arm, more like a snake than a fish, and it scowled up at him with needle-point eyes and razor-sharp teeth.

"You shouldn't swear like that, Young Lambton," came a warning voice from behind him. "Especially on a Sunday."

The boy spun round, and there he saw an old man, his face all cracked and pitted and his clothes little more than rags.

"Don't creep up on me like that, you old beggar," cried the boy. "And anyway, who gives a damn about Sundays? It's just another day when people tell you what to do and what not to do, and I'm fed up with it! Fed up with all of them!"

Young Lambton turned to take another look at his catch, which was lashing its tail this way and that in a desperate effort to free itself. "If you want to be useful, whoever you are, tell me what this thing is on the end of my line. It looks like the devil, and smells even worse!"

The man came closer. "You're right, it does stink, and it's an ugly-looking brute ..."

"Nearly as ugly and smelly as you!" replied the boy, with a laugh. "But what is it, old man, and where does it come from?"

The man came up close and then pulled away, gasping.

"What's wrong?" said Young Lambton, for the old fellow's face had gone from a dirty brown to a pale white.

"There's only one thing it can be ..." came the reply, "and it's a bad day that brings it onto land."

"Why? What is it?"

"It comes from deep down in the river," the man told him, "and that's where it should have stayed, lad – if you hadn't been down here fishing when you ought to have been in church, like everyone else."

Chapter 2
The Worm of the Wild

"If the monster comes from the river, then that's where it should go back!" said Young Lambton. And he went to pull the evil-looking worm from the line and fling it to the deep-down bottom of the river.

"No!" The man grabbed his arm. "You can't!"

"Why not?"

"Because it's a Worm of the Wild and it's wicked, at that," came the reply. "There'll be trouble for the person who catches it."

"All the more reason to toss it back in!" said Young Lambton.

"Ah, but you can't," repeated the man. "That's the problem."

"You're the problem!" cried the boy. "Now clear off and let me get on with my life!"

"All you care about is yourself, lad ..." The man spoke slowly, in the hope that the boy would pay attention to his words. "But there's more than you in the world, Young Lambton, and if you do things you shouldn't, you have to pay the price."

"Away with you, you old beggar!" The boy waggled the foul-smelling fish in his face. "Away with you and your stupid warnings."

The man gave him a cold, hard look in return. "I'll go in my own time," he said. "But take note of what I say, boy – watch what you do with that Worm, for he who catches it must keep it. If you put it back, now you've taken it from the water, it'll bring down a terrible curse upon you and your people."

Young Lambton had stopped listening to the old man. He turned his back on him, and stuck out his tongue at the nasty-looking thing on the end of his line, instead – which stared back at him with its cold, angry eyes.

"And as for you …" he told the monster. "Don't think I'm hanging on to you one second longer than I need to, you great fat maggot!"

He shook his line out over the water, trying to return the creature to the river. But no matter how hard he shook it, the thing wouldn't budge.

"Fair enough. I'll toss you down the well instead," he said. And he set off towards his home, holding the Worm as far away from him as he could.

When he came to the well, Young Lambton poked his fishing rod down the hole. Then he took out his knife and cut the line, so the wiggly jiggly ugly thing dropped deep down into the coal-black darkness.

"Bye bye, you brute," said the boy.

But somehow the old man was standing behind him again. "I warned you, lad!" he said. "And now there's nothing more to be done. The creature is free to wander the land, and the Curse of the Worm is upon you!"

Chapter 3
Terror in the Dark

The Worm was a nasty, greedy thing, eating everything in sight. It ate slugs, snails, frogs and toads, it gobbled the weeds and it gulped down the water. And as the well got emptier, the monster got bigger.

Until one day it was too big to fit inside the well any more, and too hungry to want to stay there. With a burp and a fart and a great slimy heave, it forced itself up and out and over the edge.

Blinking in the light, sniffing the air, it turned towards the river and slithered its way home.

It plopped in, slurping down great gallons of water and gobbling up every living thing it saw. Then it crawled back out onto a rock in the middle of the river, coiled itself three times around it and fell asleep.

But the monster was so large by now that by night it was hungry again. It slipped out of the river, in search of more food, and spotted a great heavy cow, standing alone in a field. As silent as the stars, the Worm slithered through the grass and when it reached the poor cow, it wrapped itself around it and sucked all the milk out of it.

The next night it ate three sheep, and all the farmer found was their skins. The villagers took to shutting their animals away before dark after that, to try and protect

them. But the Worm wasn't afraid of light, or of being seen. It slipped out of the river, well before nightfall, and when the people saw it they ran for their homes, locking their doors and blocking up their windows.

Often there was no time to shut their animals away, so the creature ate as many as it wanted. It sucked down the cows' milk, gobbled up the tasty little lambs, and returned to its rock in the middle of the river to sleep.

"I'm sorry!" cried Young Lambton, when he found out what was going on, and that he was the cause of it. "I'm sorry I didn't go to church! I'm sorry I swore and was rude to you, Father! I'm sorry I threw the creature into the well and brought down the Curse of the Worm upon us!"

But it was way too late for sorry. The old man he'd met by the river had been right, and it looked like no one would sleep soundly ever again.

"I shall go away," vowed Young Lambton. "I shall travel the world as a poor man, begging forgiveness for my sins, and maybe the Worm will leave you all in peace." And then he had another thought. "Or maybe he'll follow me," he said, a shiver running through him. "Maybe I'll never be free of him, wherever I go ..."

He packed his bags and his father cried to see him leave. *But at least,* thought Lord Lambton, *my people might be safe again.*

Chapter 4
Knight Attack

But they weren't safe. For that evening the hungry Worm slithered out of the river, and it didn't stop in the fields. No, it made its foul and horrible way up to the Hall itself. The people locked themselves into the kitchens, piling up tables and chairs against the doors. Then they armed themselves with anything they could lay their hands on – knives and hammers, spades and pick-axes. Although they knew, deep down, that they'd be little use against the might of the Worm if it made up its mind to come and get them.

It didn't need to, though, not that night anyway, for there were enough animals left outside the kitchens to satisfy its hunger. It ate every dog and every cat it could find, and the only one to escape was old Mullet, Young Lambton's favourite hound.

Every evening the monster came, and every evening it brought terror with it. Until an old servant came up with an idea. He'd worked out cows seemed to be the thing it liked most of all to feed on. "Bring your buckets!" he called to the milkmaids. "Don't waste a drop!"

He told them to pour all the milk from the last nine cows into the great stone trough in front of Lambton Hall.

And when the Worm came that evening it stopped, sniffed the air, and went straight to

the trough. It guzzled the lot, splashing away greedily, and when every last drop was gone and it had licked the stones all around, it slithered back down to the river, full and happy.

Every afternoon from then on the milkmaids filled up the trough with the milk from the last remaining cows, and every evening the Worm came and guzzled. It slurped and it burped and it left without harm.

As long as there was enough to satisfy its hunger, it was fine. But if ever there was less than the milk of nine cows – if the maids had spilt some, or if any of the cows were sick and not able to be milked – the Worm would hiss and snarl, tear out trees by their roots and then slither off to find something else to feast on.

Lord Lambton was desperate. His land was spoiled, most of his animals were dead and his only son had left him. And he knew, too, that in time the cows would no longer be able to produce milk. The Worm would go crazy and nothing but nothing would escape its rage.

He put out the word across all the land that whoever could kill the mighty creature would be given half of all his fortune.

"I will save you!" cried a brave young knight, riding in from the Far Lands.

He hid under the trough until the monster came up to drink. And when it opened its huge, dark cave of a mouth, the knight rolled out from underneath, drew out his shining sword and plunged it deep down its throat.

What's this? thought the Worm. *The tickling of a toothbrush?*

It looked around, saw its attacker and lashed out with its tail, winding it around him. Then it drew him in tighter and tighter until the poor man popped out of his armour. Tighter still the Worm squeezed, until the very life was squeezed out of the brave young knight. And then the creature gobbled him up as a tasty starter, washing him down with the milk.

"I will save you and your people, Lord Lambton!" cried a second young knight. And he waited by the river for the Worm to come out.

With a mighty blow the brave warrior chopped it in two, but to his horror the two ends of the creature grew back together, even stronger than before.

The Worm took one look at the skinny little knight and pounced. Then it crushed him, munched him and burped.

Five knights came. Ten knights came. But no matter how many attacked the Worm, no matter how many pieces they hacked off it, the creature came back together, stronger and fiercer. The knights ran off, screaming for mercy, and those that were caught were gobbled up and gulped down.

Chapter 5
The Lambton Curse

After seven years, Young Lambton returned home. Never once on his travels did he come across the Worm or hear word of it, so that he came to believe that he had been right to go, that the curse had lifted, and that the creature had returned to its home at the bottom of the river.

Coming over the hill, though, Young Lambton was horror-struck at what he saw. The land was destroyed, the trees were flattened, the animals lay dying and his father, when he met him, was furious.

"Where have you been, you good-for-nothing son? Have you any idea how terrible it has been for us here?"

"I'm sorry, Father." Young Lambton was amazed at how old and sad his father looked. "I thought that by leaving, I would take the curse with me."

His father told him of all that had happened, of how all his servants had deserted him or been killed, and of the death of the knights who tried to tackle the Worm.

"It's my fault that all this happened," cried Young Lambton. "And now that I am home, it is up to me to sort it out, for once and for all!"

He went down to the river to take a look at the foul creature, and who should appear

but the old man he'd met so long ago, even greyer and more wrinkled than before.

"You were right when you told me that it was my problem and mine alone," said Young Lambton. "But our people have suffered enough for my mistake. What can I do?"

The old man looked at him long and hard. "You have learnt your lesson, Young Lambton, and you have come to the right person. For you alone can kill this Worm, and only I can tell you how."

"Tell me," begged the desperate young man, "for I must save my people!"

"I will," came the reply. "Listen carefully."

Young Lambton sat at his feet, and the withered old man told him what to do.

"You must not fight the Worm on land," he said, "but stand on its rock in the middle of the river, attacking it while it is still in the water."

"I will do as you say," said the youth.

"Also you must ask the blacksmith to make you the most deadly suit of armour that he can. It must be covered, all around the outside, with the sharpest blades and spikes that have ever been made."

"It will be done," said Young Lambton, turning to go.

"Wait!" cried the old man. "There is one more thing you must do, or all your efforts will be wasted."

"What's that?" asked Young Lambton.

"You must swear an oath, here and now, that when you finally kill the Worm you will then also kill the next living thing you meet."

Young Lambton frowned, not understanding.

"If you do not do as I say," the old man warned him, "the Curse of the Worm will become a curse upon your whole family, now and forever!"

"What do you mean?" The boy's face went white.

"I mean that the Lords of Lambton, their sons and their sons' sons for the next nine generations, will each die a terrible death. Not a single one will pass away peacefully in his bed."

The young man realised he had no choice but to agree. "I do not like the sound of this promise," he said, "but if it is the only way to make sure that the Worm is dead forever, and that my family will survive, then I will swear to it."

When he returned to the Great Hall he went down to the blacksmith, ordering him to make him up the finest and deadliest suit of armour, all studded with razor-sharp spear points. He asked him also to forge the strongest, sharpest sword the land had ever seen.

While the blacksmith was working, Young Lambton made his way to the church, where he prayed for the courage to challenge the Worm and the strength to defeat it. He prayed also that he would be forgiven for what he had to do after he had killed it. For he understood now what the promise he had given to the old man would mean, and he knew how hard it would be to obey it and how much sadness it would bring.

When the blacksmith's job was completed, he helped Young Lambton into his armour, taking great care not to be stabbed by the deadly spikes. Then off went the Lord's son to tell his father that he was going out to kill the Worm.

"When you hear me blow on my horn, you will know that it is dead," the young man told him. "You must open the door of the hall and let my good dog Mullet run to greet me. Mullet, and not anyone else," he insisted. "Will you do that, Father? Do you promise?"

Mullet, hearing his name, came running, and Young Lambton stroked him fondly.

"You're a good dog," he said, with a note of sadness in his voice.

The Lord agreed to do as he'd been asked, but his son hadn't the heart to explain the reason, not wanting to worry his father any more than he was worried already.

Chapter 6
The Final Battle

When the Worm came up to the Hall to feed, Young Lambton slipped past him. He swam out to its rock and waited.

All around him was silent, but he knew that the challenge that faced him was the greatest challenge of his life – the greatest that any Lambton had ever faced. He feared it, but knew there was no other way – he had to make up for his stupidity as a boy if his people were to survive.

The Worm, returning home fat and full, spotted him as it entered the water. Bellowing with rage at the sight of an intruder on its rock, it smashed its tail hard on the water. Great waves broke over the rock, and Young Lambton could hardly stop himself from sliding into the crashing water.

The monster made a dive for him, but the youth was quicker. Raising his brand-new sword, he brought it crashing down on the Worm's tail. The creature squealed, the tail broke off and, to Young Lambton's delight, floated away down the river.

"Away with you, Worm," he roared, holding his sword high in the air. "For only I have the power to kill you!"

And the Worm was frightened then, for it knew it had met a true rival at last. One who had the strength to chop off its limbs in such a way that they would never grow again.

The monster snarled and then pounced. Wrapping its head and body around Young Lambton, it aimed to stay in close so that this knight – so much more dangerous than all the ones who had come before – couldn't get a swing at him.

But then the Worm squealed, as the deadly spikes on the young man's armour cut through its scales. It squeezed with all its might, hoping to crush the life out of its opponent before he could do any more damage. But it was useless, for the harder the Worm pressed, the deeper its flesh was stabbed by the razor-sharp blades.

Freeing his arm, the young lord slashed at the monster's body, lopping bits off, piece by piece. And each time, rather than fixing themselves back on and adding to the creature's strength, they drifted off down the blood-red river.

Without its tail to lash with, all the Worm could do was carry on squeezing. It tried biting great lumps out of any part of Young Lambton it could reach, but he was always too quick for it.

Coiling and crushing, the creature still hoped to finish his opponent off, but the tighter it squeezed, the more it ripped itself to pieces on his spikes.

At last the monster could squeeze no more, for all its strength was gone. It pulled away from Young Lambton, hoping to escape before further damage was done. But it was too late and too slow. The knight raised his sword high in the air, brought it crashing down on the exhausted creature, and sliced the monster in two.

With a final sickening roar, both halves of the Worm slipped into the water and sank to the bottom of the river.

Alone on the rock, filled with pride, the young man drew out his horn and blew it three times. Then he lowered himself into the blood-red water and swam to shore.

"My son!" cried Lord Lambton, hearing the call. "He is alive!"

Rushing to the door of the Hall, he threw it open and ran down the garden to greet him.

"No, Father!" cried the knight, horror-struck at the sight before him. "I warned you!"

"What? You warned me what?" For Lord Lambton, in the joy of knowing that his son had saved them from the Worm, had completely forgotten the promise he'd made.

"I warned you to send the dog out first, before anyone else!"

"Why?" The old man was confused. "What does it mean?"

Young Lambton looked up at him. He knew that the Curse of the Worm meant that he had no choice now but to kill his very own father. And he knew that it was impossible.

"Go back inside," he gasped. "Send out my old dog Mullet, instead."

"May I be forgiven for what I am about to do," muttered the blood-spattered knight. And when his faithful hound came bounding towards him, he raised his sword high.

The old dog, trusting as ever, just carried on running, and Young Lambton, with the very last of his strength, buried the blade between poor Mullet's eyes.

"What have you done, my son?" cried his father, rushing back out.

Young Lambton gasped out an explanation and they held each other close, in relief and sorrow.

The Worm was finally dead, and the seven years of terror were over. But it was not enough to have killed Mullet, as Young Lambton knew. The promise that he had made to the old man he'd met down by the river was broken, meaning that the Curse of the Worm was no longer just upon him but upon his whole family, until the end of time.

And from that day on, until the name died out forever, every first-born son of the Lambtons died the most horrible of deaths.

The Legend

The Lambton Worm is one of the most popular legends from the North East of England. John Lambton was heir to the Lambton Estate in County Durham. He is supposed to have had a battle with a giant Worm which had been terrorising local villages.

It is said that, just as the curse of the Worm foretold, no first-born son of the Lambtons, over the next nine generations, died peacefully in his bed. We don't know what happened to Young Lambton himself, but here are some we do know about:

Robert Lambton, Young Lambton's first-born son, drowned.

Sir William Lambton was killed at the battle of Marston Moor.

Another William Lambton died in battle at Wakefield.

And the last Lambton, Henry, died in a horse-drawn carriage, crossing Lambton Bridge in 1761.

Malachy Doyle

Author

Favourite hero:
Albert Buggins.

Favourite monster:
My brother Jim.

Secret power:
I know how to spell "porridge" (which I have every morning for breakfast).

Favourite fight scene:
The one where my brother Jim tries to eat my porridge and, thanks to a little help from Albert Buggins, it ends up all over him.

Goodie or baddie:
A goodie pretending to be a baddie pretending to be a goodie.

RELOADED

Dylan Gibson

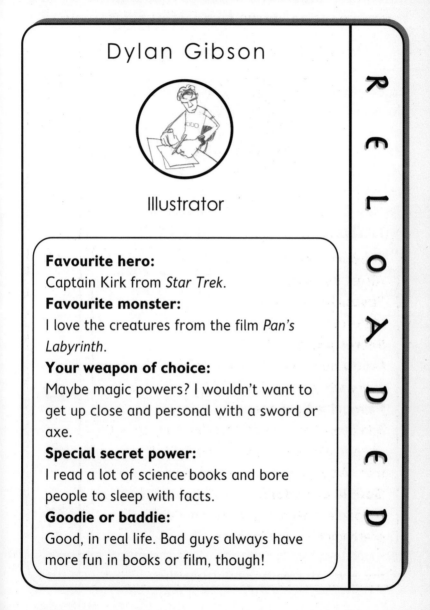

Illustrator

Favourite hero:
Captain Kirk from *Star Trek*.

Favourite monster:
I love the creatures from the film *Pan's Labyrinth*.

Your weapon of choice:
Maybe magic powers? I wouldn't want to get up close and personal with a sword or axe.

Special secret power:
I read a lot of science books and bore people to sleep with facts.

Goodie or baddie:
Good, in real life. Bad guys always have more fun in books or film, though!

RELOADED

Become a Consultant!

THE NIGHT OF THE KELPIES

BY
JOAN LENNON

Sandy bets that he can spend the night at the Bay.
It's supposed to be haunted by Kelpies – evil sea
creatures that take humans as slaves – but Sandy
doesn't believe that rubbish.

Until midnight strikes.

And the Queen of the Kelpies comes for him …

You can order *The Night of the Kelpies* directly from
www.barringtonstoke.co.uk

THE GHOST OF SHADOW VALE

BY
JONATHAN STROUD

Glam killed the monster of Shadow Vale –
but he also died in the fight.
Now Glam's ghost has come back.
Grettir is the strongest man in the land.
But how can Grettir kill a dead man?

You can order *The Ghost of Shadow Vale* directly from
www.barringtonstoke.co.uk

MEET TOM YAMADA.

HE'S 15.
HE EATS JUNK FOOD
HE PLAYS NINTENDO.
HE SPENDS SEVERAL
HOURS EVERY DAY
TRAINING TO SAVE THE
WORLD.

TOM MUST BATTLE THE
5 LORDS OF PAIN
ONE BY ONE.

FIVE DEMONS.
ONE WARRIOR.
NO SECOND CHANCES.

Check out Tom's first duel in ...

The Lord of the Mountain

Tom Yamada must fight the demon Lords of Pain in a series of duels called the Contest – with the whole world at stake.

The first duel

Tom faces the Lord of the Mountain. Three metres tall, three eyes, one hell of a temper...

For more info check out www.fivelordsofpain.co.uk or www.barringtonstoke.co.uk